D0502882

RONAN
THE
LIBRARIAN

To mighty librarians and fierce booksellers everywhere
—T.L. and B.C.

To Federico, for inspiring me every day
—V.M.

Published by Roaring Brook Press
Roaring Brook Press is a division of Holtzbrinck Publishing Holdings Limited Partnership
120 Broadway, New York, NY 10271
mackids.com

Library of Congress Control Number: 2019941012

ISBN: 978-1-250-18921-9

Our books may be purchased in bulk for promotional, educational, or business use.
Please contact your local bookseller or the Macmillan Corporate and
Premium Sales Department at (800) 221-7945 ext. 5442 or by email at
MacmillanSpecialMarkets@macmillan.com.

First edition, 2020
Book design by Aram Kim
Printed in China by Hung Hing Off-set Printing Co. Ltd.,
Heshan City, Guandong Province

1 3 5 7 9 10 8 6 4 2

RONAN THE LIBRARIAN

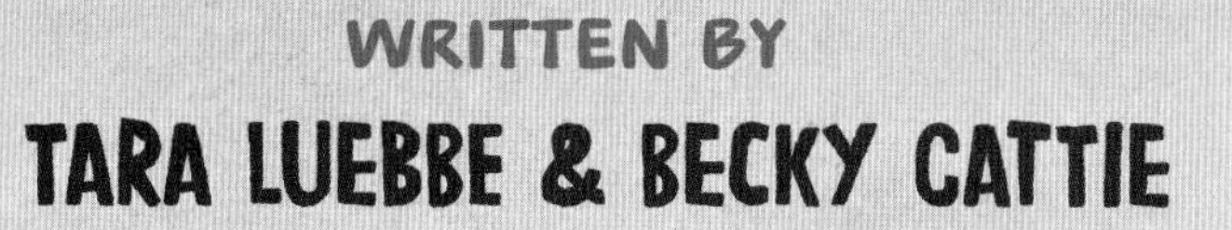

WRITTEN BY
TARA LUEBBE & BECKY CATTIE

ILLUSTRATED BY
VICTORIA MADERNA

ROARING BROOK PRESS
NEW YORK

Ronan was a mighty barbarian—a leader of his people.

He invaded.

He raided.

And back home, he traded.

Ronan was legendary for finding the best pillage—
gold, jewelry, weapons, and tools.
Everyone wanted to trade with him.

Until one raid went horribly wrong.
"What's this?" he roared. "This is worthless!"

Ronan tried to barter, but no one would make a deal.

Barbarians didn't read books.

Ronan took the book home.

"Uff da! What am I going to do with this useless thing?"

Then a picture caught his eye.

Ronan read the first sentence. Then a paragraph. Then a page.

Before he knew it, he had devoured an entire chapter.

He read until the moon was high in the sky.

The next day, Ronan didn't meet the raiding party.

"He must have overslept," said Krom. "Let's go wake him."

"Ronan, you dunga! What are you doing?" asked Gunnar.

"I'm reading," Ronan said. "This book is epic. Do you want to borrow it?"

"Have you gone berserk? Barbarians don't read. We raid!" said Helgi.

His friends were right.

Ronan tucked the book away and went raiding, like a good barbarian.

But he couldn't stop thinking about the book.

When the raid was over, he charged home and read straight through to the end.

Ronan was hooked. He needed a new book.

So he invaded and raided and read.

He invaded and raided and read.

He invaded and raided and read.

The fierce raider became a fierce reader, and soon his massive collection threatened to devour him.

So Ronan came up with a solution to tame the beast: He built a library.

He even threw a grand-opening celebration!

But . . .

Barbarians do not read books.

Krom judged the books by their covers.

Gunnar valued brawn over brains.

Helgi was too busy to read.

How could Ronan get his people to see that books were treasures?

"Uff da! I must conquer my own village," he declared.

He picked up his book, held it high, and began to read aloud.

“The troll roared as Odin snatched the Urn of Unkar and raced to his ship. The crew rowed out to sea when out of the depths rose the terrifying kraken.

"Odin held on to the urn for dear life as he drew his sword . . ."

But the shipbuilders continued sawing.

The blacksmiths didn't stop hammering.

And the potters kept on spinning their wheels.

It was a crushing defeat.

At daybreak, Ronan went to his library.

"Uff da! I've been invaded!"

LIBRARY

WELCOME
“And raided!”
What was in the urn?

It was his greatest victory yet.

THE LIBRARY WAS FULL OF BARBARIANS!

Ronan quickly laid down the law.

He issued library cards, he recommended books,

and he read to the younglings.

It turns out, barbarians *do* read books.

BOOKISH BARBARIANS
BOOK CLUB
READERS MAKE BETTER RAIDERS

Ronan was a mighty librarian—a leader of his people.

They invaded.

They raided.

They read.